DEVIL'S TALE

LUNA KAYNE

We have never heard the devil's side of the story,
God wrote all the book.

— ANATOLE FRANCE

CHAPTER 1
AHNA

If I get pulled over by one more patrol car *'just checking to make sure that little ol' me is okay on these dark and scary backroads'*, I'm going to tear this county a new one.

My inhale is slow and forced to calm the disdain bubbling inside of me. When I release my frustrations for this godforsaken place, it comes out in a steady flow through pinched lips.

The truth is: I need these backroads. I have to stay off the main streets and out of crowded areas. I'm sure my absence has been noticed by now, and I'd just end up getting into trouble.

Leaning over to glance at the map on the passenger seat, I double check the pen markings I added to make sure my shortcut doesn't end up getting me lost.

It looks like there's a main highway coming up in about ten miles. Outside of the gas station I filled up at thirty minutes ago, I haven't passed a single building for miles.

A solid thud against my grill sends chills through my body.

A surprised squeal leaves my lips as I tighten my grip on the wheel and snap my attention to the darkened dirt road just in time to watch a deer launch up my hood into the windshield before launching over the roof.

In a panic, I step my foot hard on the brake. Forgetting my foot is on the gas, I speed up and turn my wheel as hard as I can.

Closing my eyes tight and bracing every muscle for impact, the poor animal yowls as it bounces up and over my roof, and rocks spray out as I veer off the road into the ditch.

When the impact never comes, I open my eyes slowly to a cloud of dust all around the car and the sound of a country song cracking through the radio.

There's something to be said for open prairie farmlands, at least there's no cliff to go hurtling off of.

Throwing the car into reverse, I attempt to get out the way I got in, but the car only rocks weakly as the tires spin, catching on nothing. I must have wedged myself against something in the ditch.

Where the hell are all of those small town sheriffs that were all up in my grill before?, I wonder to myself as I push open the door to my little sedan. I could really use the help now.

Stepping out and crouching by the back tire of my car confirms my assumption. I managed to land right on top of the only large boulder in this ditch and I won't be able to haul my car off.

It doesn't matter. I'm close enough that a little walk late at night on a deserted road might do me good.

What's the worst that could happen, in the middle of nowhere on Halloween night? The clouded breath that leaves with my thought sends a shiver down my spine, and I catch myself before I let fear replace my bravado.

I'm better than this.

Reaching into the back seat, I grab an old blanket left behind by the vehicle's previous owner.

With the radio now off, there's no other sound around me which doesn't bode well for the deer I hit.

I walk back through the tall grass to check on the animal silently wishing it's just stunned. My hopes are dashed when I find the poor creature thirty feet behind the car, dead.

Even I can muster some empathy for this poor creature and I cover the carcass with the blanket.

Scanning both directions the road goes in, I weigh my options. I know I should start walking, and there's no point in heading back in the direction I came from. There's nothing back there for me.

My future lies on the road ahead. I feel it in my bones like an incessant whisper refusing to quiet.

The cool night air steadies my nerves. I take one last look at the road I just traveled before turning to walk in the direction I was originally headed in with nothing but the silent stars above to guide my way.

***

Three miles into my trek with nothing but crickets and the occasional animal howl to keep me company, a little house in the middle of nowhere finally appears. It's so displaced among the patches of forest and open farm land that I stop to stare at it for a few minutes longer, daring it to vanish before my eyes like a mirage.

But it doesn't.

The porch light is on and smoke billows from the chimney stack.

Someone is inside.

The cold night air set in a while ago and I've been shivering uncontrollably for the last fifteen minutes.

As I near the steps of the little house I'm oddly struck by the decorations that line the walkway to the front door. Carved pumpkins with candles light a little path as though the owner of this place expects trick-or-treaters all of the way out here.

I stop at the edge of the yard to look at the lit path, then turn and take one last look at the landscape around me. Not one light dots the horizon.

I'm still as far from civilization as I can get.

The porch is lit with a lantern and an old wooden swing slowly creaks as it sways with a wind I don't feel on my skin.

With no doorbell to ring, I clench my cold fingers together and knock as loud as I can with the side of my fist hoping I'm not waking anyone up.

A half minute passes and I'm almost ready to knock again when the floorboards on the other side of the thin door creak then thud with the distinct sound of footsteps.

Then the front door opens and I take a half step back in the warm light.

The make eye contact with the man who's now looking at me with a half smile, my stomach does a little flip and my heart feels light. I'm not one to believe in love at first sight but this guy is making me rethink some things.

Maybe it's just horny at first sight. It has been awhile.

The thought flies around my head and I momentarily forget why I'm standing on the porch of a house in the middle of nowhere on tonight of all nights with my hand raised into a fist as though I'm actually going to knock again.

"Aren't you a little old to be out here looking for candy?" His amused tone draws me in even more than the sight of his firm muscles peeking out from the sleeves of his tight fitted shirt.

"I—um—ha!" I snort out a chuckle and recover with a deep breath, feeling suddenly light headed. I've never in my life been one to get tongue tied and I'm not going to start now. Quickly regaining my composure, I smile then point in the direction I came from. "No, I'm not here for candy. My car broke down a few miles down the road and—"

His eyes travel to my extended arm as it trembles and I realize the cold has taken over as he cuts me off.

"You're shivering, you must be freezing. Why don't you have a warm jacket?" He looks around my person, then behind me. "You're all the way out her and you have nothing with you?"

"I didn't expect to break down out here." My voice sounds more meek than I intend as I shrug my shoulders, now realizing I probably should have kept the blanket for myself instead of leaving it with an animal that doesn't need it.

"You should know by now that life never happens as you expect it to. You should be better prepared." His words wrap around me as his voice takes on a deeper, almost chastising tone.

"You're right. Lesson learned. Do you have a phone I could use? I lost battery in mine an hour ago."

"It wouldn't matter anyway. There's no cell out here. You broke down about as far away from anywhere as you could, Miss—?" His words linger mid-sentence.

Then I realize he's looking for a name before he lets me into his house.

"Ahna. I'm Ahna." I rock on my heels and hope I don't look foolish.

"Ana?" He repeats, incorrectly.

"No, Ahna. Like 'awww, isn't she cute'." I immediately shut my mouth hoping that last sentence didn't really just come out of it.

"Awww, isn't—she—cute, Awwwna." His words are low and slow—so seductively slow.

The smile that crosses his lips is predatory. I sense he's playing with me and I kind of like it. Even the shiver his tone sends through me is warming me right up.

Wait. What?

"Um, yeah. That's it." I meet his gaze for a fraction of a second then lose my courage when he licks his lip and lower my eyes, settling on his lips as he speaks.

"That's a beautiful name, Ahna. I'm Jake. So Ahna, with the broken down car and light summer jacket on such a cold night, what can I do for you?" A jolt of energy zaps through me as my brain starts to mentally list off all of the things he could do for me.

Luckily my mouth has separated from my thoughts as I answer him. "I was hoping I could use your phone and maybe come in and warm up for a bit."

"You can come in and get warm, but you can't use the phone. There's no service out here by land or cell. It's no use anyway. It's a Saturday night and Halloween on top of that. Tow trucks and garages won't be open until Monday mornin'."

Stepping back from the doorway to let me enter he raises his arm, pointing me into his home. I know I should be cautious, but my toes are becoming painfully cold. I step into his main room and am suddenly hit with a welcoming warmth.

Small talk isn't a strength of mine. "You decorated your yard all of the way out here. Why go through the trouble if no one shows up?" I enter into a living room and turn to face him.

"You showed up." His retort catches me off guard and I snort out a laugh.

"Well, yeah. But you weren't expecting me."

"Are you sure about that, Ahna?" He smiles, gesturing to the couch in the middle of the room and a chill runs down my spine. Catching my hesitation, he continues, "Remember, expect the unexpected in life." Then he chuckles, and I realize it is at my expense as I stand here gawking at him with my mouth open.

"Have a seat. I just made some tea. There should be enough for two. I'll be right back." As he turns to leave, the quiet around the room sets in.

There really is no one else around.

I slip out of my shoes and leave them by the door then make my way further into the house to explore.

The house holds warmth but lacks personality. No photos or knick knacks line the shelfs. The one painting in the room seems detached from the area it occupies. Everything feels as out of place as his house does, out here in the middle of nowhere.

Another phantom shiver runs through me.

I stretch out my arms and shake off the cold as Jake returns, carrying two mugs with delightful wafts of steam rising from the tops.

"I hope lemon chamomile tea is okay. It's all I've got." He hands a mug to me and sits down on the sofa.

"Thank you. It's fine." I take a seat on the other side of the sofa, angling my body to face him.

I lift my mug up to my face and close my eyes to smell the tea and the heat pokes at my cold nose causing me to sniffle. I open my eyes to find Jake sitting still, watching me.

"So why are you travelling down these deserted roads? And on Halloween no less. I'm pretty sure that's how most horror movies start." He kisses his lips together, blowing on his drink.

I follow his hands as he rests his cup on his lap and try to think of an answer that doesn't make me sound like a lunatic.

"My landlord kicked me out of my place without warning. I have a friend a couple of hours away I'm going to stay with until I can figure something out." I take a sip of my tea. The hot sting on my tongue tells me it isn't cooled yet. Or maybe it's my penance for lying through my teeth.

"That seems unfair." His eyebrows knit together, and I deepen my little white lie to make it more believable.

Shrugging my shoulders I drop my focus down to my mug. "Well, when I don't pay rent for a few months—" I trail off and pause for dramatic effect. "I got laid off from my last job."

"I see." The tone of his voice dances between concern and chiding and I change the subject.

"Why should I be concerned with traveling tonight?" I take my first real sip of my tea and it tastes delicious, warming me from the inside out.

"Haven't you heard that the devil goes hunting for his mate on Halloween?" He asks, then follows me in taking a sip, and I notice he hasn't taken his eyes off me.

If this is his way of flirting with me, I'm all in.

Trailing my eyes down his torso, I can only imagine how hard his abs are and how much I'd love to sink my teeth into his—

"Ahna?" His voice holds a hint of humor, but my name finally catches my attention and I realize, too late, that I missed something.

"I'm sorry. I've been driving a little too long and I'm tired. My mind must have wandered. What did you say?"

He smirks as if to say he's not buying my excuse at all but he doesn't push it.

"I was just asking if you've heard the old tale about the devil and Halloween."

I've heard them all, but I don't tell him that. Instead I shrug my shoulders. "I've heard many fairy tales. What is this one about?" I hold my attention on the hot cup nestled in my hands.

"About the deal he struck with the angels. He is stripped of his powers and allowed out of Hell every one hundred years to search for his soul's true mate on one special night ,and if he finds his soulmate, he has until dawn to consummate their connection. Then they will be together forever. If not, he returns to reign over Hell alone for another century."

I smile to myself and he returns a smile to me. My family never taught me a thing. Growing up, I was always the outcast, the black sheep. I never fit in anywhere. As rash and crazy as it sounds though, I feel like I fit in here, with Jake.

Bringing myself back to the conversation, I decide to question this little tale of his.

"Surely the devil's soulmate won't want to spend an eternity in Hell."

He considers my statement with a sly smirk. "But if they are soulmates, something as minuscule as location shouldn't get in their way. If you could be with the one who knew you inside and out. Who indulged in your darkest fantasies, and loved you through your deepest secrets. Someone who was your sanctuary, your haven. The one person who personified complete love and acceptance. Would you not follow them anywhere?"

I lose myself in his words. His voice leads me down a path, and I follow his words like breadcrumbs leading me home.

Promises of everything I've ever wanted.

I've worked hard, and I've survived my entire life. I played the parts I was expected to play, and all I've ever wanted for myself is everything he just said.

I get the feeling his questions were redundant yet I whisper my answer anyway. "Yes, I would."

His soul speaks to me and I'm close to leaning in and closing my eyes when a sudden rush of heat hits me.

I realize too late that the heat is coming from the tea I just spilled all over myself in my haze.

Jumping off the couch in unison, Jake reaches for my cup and steps back from me to give me space to assess the damage.

Luckily I was near the end of my drink and only a small amount soaked through my pants.

"Are you hurt?" His eyes jump between my own and my wet spot, and heats my face no doubt flushing my cheeks.

"No. There wasn't much in my cup. It's not hot. Only bruised my ego a bit." I snort out, further punching my ticket to *Dorkville* but his smirk tells me I may have hit more of an endearing chord with him and my cheeks heat up under his gaze.

I don't blush. This is new.

"May I use your washroom?" I ask, hoping to find a few minutes to compose myself before I fall further and just try to jump on him.

What's coming over me?

"It's down the hall to the right. Don't go down the stairs." In my haste to leave, I catch every second or third word of his instructions as I scramble to put some distance between us.

I definitely need a couple of minutes to regroup.

"Okay, thanks." My delivery is quick but I don't care. It's become hot in here, and I need to breathe.

Moving down the hall, I find the steps he told me to go down. Turning suddenly, I skip down the stairs, reaching out for a light switch at the bottom.

"No, wait." He alls to me from upstairs, his footsteps thumping down the hall, but my mind is spinning and I just want to get into a different room from him.

Brushing my fingers along the wall at the bottom of the stairs, I find a switch and turn it on.

CHAPTER 2
AHNA

Lights flicker once then flood the room. My breath hitches in my throat as I process the sight before me, only slightly aware of the footsteps thudding down the stairs at my back.

The room is lit, but it's not bright as though the light is merely restrained within the room instead of illuminating it. The walls on all sides are the deepest shade of grey you can get without being black and dark crimson curtains are hung around the room even though there are no windows. They match the sheets draped across a large bed in the middle of the area, looking as if it is meant to be a stage for no audience.

But that's not what catches my attention.

My mind blanks at the sight of various hooks attached on one of the walls. Looking further, all the way up to the ceiling, I swallow a lump in my throat at the pulley system attached high above with heavy bolts.

I'm about to turn to face Jake when a wall of things stops me cold.

Lots of *things*.

Jumping from item to item, I can make out most of what I see. Chains, cuffs, belts, wooden paddles and what looks like different whips are each placed neatly in their own spots. The contrast of the sinister looking tools gently stored with purpose catch me off guard.

Then a large wooden X just beyond the bed pulls at something deep inside of me. I forget my situation as I move, almost entranced across the room to touch it.

The light fades away, casting shadows around me as I lift my hand, stretching my fingers to make contact with the soft leather covering the front. It's cool to the touch. This was hand made with extreme care given to each detail. The cross is thick and solid, sanded down and stained a beautiful dark oak shade, and I trace a line down one of the rich lines in the wood grain. The leather, a faded black is old and worn but it feels delightful against my skin.

The silence in the room is oddly comforting as I explore further up to the hooks attached to each end. They are wrought iron and heavy, meant to keep anything it holds. The urge to know what it would feel like to be bound to it ticks the corner of my mouth into the hint of a smile when—

"It's called a Saint Andrew's Cross." Jakes husky timber startles me back to the present and I jump, turning around and pulling my hand back to myself.

"Oh. I—um—okay." I stammer as I pull my hands into myself as though I just got caught trying to steal a cookie.

I expect him to step back and usher me out of the room, but he doesn't.

He doesn't move.

Instead, he takes me in with measured eyes. The weight of his gaze roams over every inch of me, and I will my dry mouth to fill with spit so that I can swallow away my tension.

"You're curious. Aren't you, Ahna?" The seduction in his tone is heady.

"What? No. H-how can you tell?" I have no idea what I'm even saying. I'm still trying to buy myself those couple of minutes to reset from earlier.

"Little tells, sweet angel. Your breathing has increased. It's become—heavy. You've parted your lips to take in more air." I seal my lips back together and attempt to even myself out as he smiles. "And you're still here."

"M-maybe I'm scared. Too scared to move." I retort rather pathetically.

He only offers me a humored nod.

We both know I'm lying.

"You're not scared. You're curious. You're drawn into this room. If you were scared, you'd be pale. You're flushed the loveliest shade of red." His words end in a pause, and my heart thunders into my throat as I wait, desperate for him to continue. "Tell me, Ahna, does it feel warm in here?" Jake takes a half-step toward me.

"It is warm in here. Kind of h-hot, actually." I force my dry throat to clear.

"I thought so. It's actually a lot colder than it is upstairs. I lower the heat when I'm not down here. But you don't feel cold do you?" Another half step.

Clenching my fingers together, they are warm, borderline sweaty. My breathing is out of control, and I'm sure he must notice how hard my heart has started beating. The rhythmic pounding in my ears is deafening.

"If you were an animal, I'd almost say you were in heat, little one." The surety in his words humbles me, and I lower my gaze to the floor. It must be written all over me.

There's a need settling deep into my bones, and I can't

pull it out. I never expected this level of attraction and it's building with every word he says.

I'm not frozen in place because I'm too scared to move.

I'm here because there is nowhere else I want to be.

Anxiety prickles along the nerves just beneath my skin at the thought. I feel like I don't know what I'm doing.

I feel scared.

Fear. Also a new one for me tonight. I've never been one to let fear take control.

As though he just listened into my private thoughts, he speaks again. "I feel it too. I'm extremely drawn to you, and being down here is heightening everything for me."

"I don't understand." My words break off into a thousand simultaneous thoughts my head.

Keeping my body squared on Jake, I scan the room, keeping track of where he is at all times.

He hasn't moved from his spot.

He hasn't lunged at me.

He's taller and larger than I am.

Yet he hasn't moved.

"You have a question, Ahna. Ask it."

I furrow my brow, tilting my head in morbid curiosity.

I do have a question.

I don't know how to word it but I know, in my current state, nothing is going to come out right anyway so—

"You—d-do you want to hurt me?" My tone startles me. I almost sound hopeful.

"I think you know I don't want to harm you. But I would like to watch you experience pain." The thought of me crying for him gnaws at something long since locked away, and I inhale a deep breath to regain my composure.

A tinge of triumph warms his expression on his face as he watches me.

Shifting in his stance, he continues to watch me like the predator I sense he is.

Control.

I've always been in control.

My entire life I've been the top of the food chain wherever I went. I always imagined I would end up with someone who would be more—dependent—on me. Yet I'm standing here, surrounded by everything that is designed to take my control away from me and hand it over to him.

And I feel like I'm home, like I've found my place, my purpose.

"I'm—" My words trail off as I take one more look around the room.

I take everything in a second time and I notice Jake move to the light switch and dim the lights a little more.

The edges of the room dull until they slip into shadows, and my hesitation drains out of me. As I watch him cross the area, closing the distance between us, the air becomes thick.

Jake has changed from the man I spoke with upstairs. He moves methodically toward me, sure of everything around him, and his eyes are focused and trained on my every move.

I have never know what it felt like to be someone's prey before tonight.

Stopping in front of me, he lifts his hand to place it on my neck, but stops short. Everything inside of me wants him to complete the connection. To take what he desires, but he pauses.

"Tell me you want this, Ahna. Tell me I can play with you tonight. I'll follow your lead, and I'll only give you what you need." Then leaning in, his mouth so close to my ear that his hot breath tickles my heated flesh, he whispers. "Do you want to know what it feels like to enjoy pain? Tell me I can play with you, Ahna?"

How am I still standing?

Paralyzed by his words, my insides go soft yet I don't move. The small space between his fingers and my throat becomes charged, and a hunger sets in.

"Yes, Jake. I want you to play with me. Tell me you want me." My tone drops into a husky whisper.

"More than anything. I want you, Ahna." As he says my name his fingers make contact around my throat, blazing a trail of molten heat straight into my core.

Thunder cracks across the sky outside, startling me and sending goosebumps across my sensitive body. It's muffled down here in the basement, but it sounds like a storm is coming.

Jake's hand guides my head, gently tilting my face up to meet his stare and his strength becomes soft, lulling me into him. His mouth opens enough for him to lick his tongue along his lower lip as his eyes roam over my face. He leaves a trail of wetness that my parched tongue wants to devour, and I lick my own lips in response.

The corners of his mouth twitch upward as he leans in painfully slow, and brushes his lush lips against mine.

I moan, leaning into him in an attempt to deepen the kiss but he isn't having it. He pulls back as I glare at him in frustration, and his smirk begins to test my restraint.

Lowering his tone, he draws my attention entirely to him as he speaks. "Patience. All in good time. I want to savor you." He pauses to watch my face and I wonder what he is waiting for. Slowly, so painfully slowly, he brushes his fingers up my thigh and pushes against my jeans, rubbing along my most sensitive area. I whimper then as my body relaxes at his touch. He scans my face, his gaze flitting from my eyes to my lips and back. He lowers his head closer to my own. "You're going to hurt for me, Ahna. You're going to cry. You're going to moan. You're going to beg and you're going to take pure pleasure from everything I give you."

I'm wound too tight.

My head spins with images of him taking control, taking what's his, just taking—consuming, and I want to offer myself to him. My knees buckle at the thought, and he spins me around, walking me backwards until I'm standing against the wooden cross.

"You have too much energy. I feel your anxiety taking over. I want you to settle a bit before I start with you." My hips jerk as he pulls open the top button on my pants all while keeping his eyes on mine, willing me not to look away, and I don't.

I'm his to do with as he pleases.

"Pull your pants down to your knees."

I obey his command instantly, and slide my jeans over my hips, letting them fall halfway down my legs.

His hand moves down my stomach and under the seam of my panties. The room disappears further into darkness, and I follow the sensation of his rough fingers as he glides over my mound and nestles gently into my folds. A whimper escapes me when I realize how easily he is moving along between my lips. I'm so wet and his dark chuckle tells me he knows it too.

"I want to watch you come for me. It'll calm you. Whenever you're ready, just come. You need this." He braces his free arm across my upper body, holding me down. His words throw me into compliance, and I shift my body open for him, granting him access to anything he wants.

He is entirely composed while I feel like I'm falling apart, shattering what I was to make way for what I might become. Hitting one spot on my clit, my mouth goes slack and I moan for him.

His cheek twitches, the smallest indication that he is satisfied with my reaction as he continues to focus on my sensitive area, increasing pressure.

I raise my hands, clutching at the sleeves on his shirt to steady myself as I begin to rock my hips with the motion of his fingers as they move back and forth along my slick folds.

"That's it. Just like that, little one." His praise spurs me to continue as I begin to move with more fervor. "Keep going. I want to watch you ride my hand." As his words flow into me, his fingers unexpectedly slide deep inside releasing the last shred of composure I was holding on to.

I can't contain the long groan flowing out of my mouth as I buck my hips at him, rubbing myself against his hand in search of my release.

He strengthens his grip around my neck, a reminder of who is really in control.

I am doing this because he wishes it.

Releasing an eternity of responsibility I let myself go, and follow his command. My body dances on its own as I grind against his fingers with more aggression.

Words mumble out of me.

I have no idea what I'm trying to say.

Jake's eyes flash bright with an intensity I feel in my core as he continues to hold me in place, moving his hand up to my throat before squeezing just enough to put me in the place I've been searching for.

His breath comes out in a growl.

The wet sounds of his palm hitting my pussy over and over again as I writhe against him send me into a daze.

The words he spoke rattle around in my head. *You have a question, Ahna. Ask it.*

Returning to his stare, I attempt a meek smile but my vulnerability before him shatters me. I am my base self. Needy and wanting and it's all on full display for him to witness.

His touch mercilessly pulses through my very being, consuming my patience and decimating my dignity. As his words echo through my brain, something deep inside of me lets go.

You have a question, Ahna.

My body moves as he wishes now. I've begun to follow as he's guiding me, and my orgasm hurtles toward me.

My moans become pleas as his lips curl into a carnal sneer.

He knows.

Ask it.

"May I come for you? I—I need to come...plea—" My words turn into a desperate groan as the cusp of my climax rages just out of reach.

Like a wolf with his prey in sight, he licks his lips as my body shudders and I unravel in front of him.

He finishes me off with his claim. "It is all mine, Ahna. You belong to me now. Show me how grateful you are, and come for me."

My mind implodes into one singularity.

I am everything and nothing all at once.

Pinned in place by my throat and clawing at his shirt, my orgasm tears its way out of me.

I am no longer myself.

My strangled cry pierces the room around us as everything I have to offer him rages out of me.

Moans vibrate from my throat against the palm of Jake's hand as he tightens his grip. Removing his fingers from inside of me as I ride out my final waves, he palms his hand over my entire area, fisting my sex in claim, and a second shock ripples through me.

Out of nowhere, I cry through the remainder of my release, unsure of the reason for my tears. I've never felt anything so perfect, yet I'm crying.

Loosening his grip my head drops forward onto him and I my adrenaline seeps out of me along with the aftershocks of my orgasm.

"Ssshh! You're okay." His words comfort me but I don't understand why he's reassuring me until I lift my head.

Two small streaks of water have soaked his shirt. I attempt to inhale but sniffle instead. I'm choked up and still sobbing, and embarrassment washes over me.

The sharp contrast in his personality from just minutes ago shocks me but he is exactly what I need right now as I find my own strength again.

"I'm okay." I meet his gaze as I echo his words.

His concern breaks into a smile as he tightens his arms around me, holding me in place.

He's still in control.

"I'm going to give you a moment to collect yourself before we continue." I release a sigh of relief and move to separate from him, but he refuses to release me. "Where do you think you're going?"

"Oh, I was just...maybe going to sit down." I tilt my head back to the large and very welcoming bed.

His eyes follow my gesture.

"We'll get there later. You can take a moment to yourself while I put you on my cross." Before his sentence is finished, he takes a step, walking me across the floor to the daunting contraption in the room.

I'm not disappointed in this turn of events, but my body

is floating back down to the ground and I'm having a hard time concentrating on anything right now.

He places me in front of the cross, then takes a hesitant step back from me, most likely testing my ability to stand on my own after what just happened.

Taking a deep breath, I drop my arms from him and stay in place, earning myself a pleased smile from him which fills me with pride. I don't recall the last time anyone was pleased with something I've done, and this seems like such a small thing compared to some of my accomplishments.

Reaching around to the back side of the wooden contraption, Jake unhooks some leather cuffs before returning to me.

Offering me one last glance, he raises his hands to show me what he's holding.

Worn leather binds with a soft fabric underneath are decorated with heavy iron clasps. As I look at the clasps, my mind wanders up to the iron hooks on the cross and my eyes follow.

That is where he plans to put me.

"I imagine you feel a little dazed, Ahna. Are you with me?" Each time he speaks it feels like a beacon in my psyche.

I latch onto his words.

He focuses me.

"Yes. I'm good." Even the tone in my voice is compliant.

"Good. I'm going to put you in place here. I'll give you some time to adjust." Squaring himself in front of me he bends a little at his knees and draws my focus to him. "This is important. I need you to know that you are choosing this, Ahna. You can stop at any time if it isn't what you want. You will not speak unless I ask you a direct question or you need to stop. We're going to do this like traffic lights. If you want me to stop completely, say *red*. If you need a moment to breath but want to continue, say *yellow*. I will ask you at different times if you are okay. I need to know you are still responsive. You will answer me by saying *green* if you wish to continue. Do you understand?"

I'm a few seconds behind his words as I take in everything, so there is a pause when he asks his question, but it isn't awkward. Jake simply smiles and waits for me to nod at him in response.

"Are you okay to continue?" He stands a fraction taller, his expression morphing into dominant control.

"Y-yes. I am."

Freezing in place, he watches me, waiting, and I knit my brows together. I've missed something. Then I wince at myself, and answer with a sheepish smile. "Green."

"Very good, Ahna. Now let's get you out of these clothes and into something a little prettier. Shirt and pants off." I waste no time in pulling my shirt up and over my head, letting it drop to the floor.

I must look a little too eager, but I don't care. Everything Jake has done since the second I wandered into the basement has been exactly what I need. I bend over and pull my jeans the rest of the way down from my knees and off with my socks.

Tucking three of the cuffs under his arm, he lifts my first wrist then goes to work wrapping the one cuff in his hand around and clasping it in place. It's decadently soft against my skin. Finishing my second wrist, he drops to his knees fastening them the same way around each ankle then slowly stands to look at his work.

"You're so beautiful like this, Ahna." I want to smile at his words but my face drops. The sincerity on his face punches into my heart.

I stand, motionless watching his eyes trail across my body, landing on each cuff and my skin prickles as goosebumps form in the wake of his stare.

"Stay."

His one word roots me to the floor and I wait in silence, watching him move to a thin dresser along one of the walls.

Opening the top drawer, he reaches in and something clanks softly in his hand as he returns to me.

With his free hand, he draws a line on my skin starting at my neck and tracing down to my breast and my nipples pebble under my bra at the sensation.

Reaching one hand behind me, the clasp is released on the first try and I'm a little impressed because I have to fight with this thing on a good day.

Returning to the front, he's not gentle as he grabs the material on my bra and pulls the straps down my arms, freeing my breasts in front of him. As I take a small step to regain my stance, he stands in front of me hungrily looking at my peaked nipples.

Reaching up, he cups my breast in his palm and releases it, then does the same on the other side.

I dizzying breeze wafts over me when a stinging slap across my nipple startles me. Gasping for air, my eyes widen and I grind my teeth together to stick to his rules of not saying a word.

This earns me an appreciative smile. I imagine he was expecting a slip from me and my confidence surges as I try to hold in a cocky smirk of my own.

Dipping his head, Jake's mouth is hot against my already heated chest and his tongue draws soothing circles around my areola, coaxing my nipples to pebble for him, and my body obeys.

Pushing closer against me, he sucks in my tight bud

forcing it up to its fullest potential. Just as I think he's about to grant me the smallest reprieve, his teeth graze against my hardened peak and he nibbles, testing my limits as I bow my body forward and whimper.

A tremor starts deep in my thighs and spreads outward until my legs are trembling, and I worry I'm about to fall over when he moves swiftly. Standing, he shows me what he's holding in his hand as he reaches around me, draping a dainty metal chain around my neck.

The metal rolls against my skin and I follow each link to its end dangling in front of me. There's a soft tug on my breast as I focus on the end piece. It looks like a—

White light fills my vision as I suck in a scream at the sudden stab of pain shooting through my nipple he was just caressing. Blinking back my tears, my body tenses and prepares to panic.

"Take deep breaths, Ahna. Stay with me. Are you okay?" I gulp air down in an attempt to calm myself and slowly open my eyes. In my shock, I hadn't realized I'd screwed them shut.

Looking from him to the source of my pain, I put my lips together and blow out a cleansing breath. My nipple is still there. It is flattened between the jaws of a tiny clamp and the pain isn't as bad as I first thought. It's just new.

Returning to meet his stare, my steady breaths return, and I nod, then whisper, "Green."

Seemingly satisfied with my response, he drops his head to my untouched breast and I fist my hands in an attempt to manage my anxiety because now I know what's coming.

Jake's hand slowly reaches for the other clamp hanging from its chain. We stare each other down as he removes the chain from around my neck. He passes the clamp under my arm and around my back so the chain linking the two clamps rests behind me.

I watch him dumbly as he focuses on my second nipple pinching it between his fingers. As he lifts the second clamp and opens it, our eyes meet for a brief moment. Breaking our connection, he lowers his gaze down to the clamp and I follow, sucking in a deep breath.

As the clamp closes down on my hardened bud the second time, I breath out in a controlled pace and allow the pain to come.

He steps aways from me as I stare down at both of my nipples, now clamped tight, and sharp jolts shoot through me as my different nerve endings are triggered.

The pain between the two is the same but different. Not knowing what was happening was better because I didn't have any anxiety, but the sudden pain and fear of the unknown was worse. Then knowing it was coming made me nervous but the pain wasn't as severe.

I giggle at my expert findings, then look up to him watching me, and I crinkle my forehead in confusion.

Why am I giggling?

"You might start feeling a little off. The brain is a funny thing. Under certain circumstances it releases a flood of chemicals into the body like adrenaline or endorphins. This is what's going to make playing together so much fun. Are you okay?"

Okay? I'm more than okay.

I'm feeling things I've never felt before and it's giving me new life.

"Green." I answer instantly.

I'm so ready to continue, I'll hook myself up to that cross if he doesn't get on with it.

"Oh, Ahna." It sounds like he's tasting my name as he

speaks it and a fierce fire kindles to life inside of me. "I do have one other thing I would love to put on you but it's too soon."

Stepping behind the cross, he pulls out a lever and slides the bottom of the X together, then latches it so it now looks more like a capital Y. The cross moves effortlessly for him, making me aware that once I am attached to the hooks, he'll be able to place me in any position he wants.

A desperate heat burns through me at the image of him in absolute control. I hold no fear for my thoughts—only intense anticipation.

Moving behind me, he nudges me forward to stand flush against the cross. His hands glide down my body and his thumbs hook into my panties, taking them down to my ankles.

He taps my foot, encouraging me to step out of my underwear for him, then he matches the hooks on my cuffs up with the hooks at the base of the wooden cross. Feeling dizzy, I reach out to hug myself steady against the solid wood and he presses the length of his body against my back, pinning me in my place.

His hands tickle against my ribs as his breath further warms the skin on my shoulder. He kisses along my back until he rests at the base of my neck. With a groan, he grinds his length into my lower back. He makes no attempt to hide his desire and it pushes me toward my breaking point.

The move is a claim, a declaration of ownership and I answer by dropping my arms to my sides in supplication. He grabs one wrist and raises it toward the top hook on the cross, then secures my second wrist in the same way.

"I'm going to move you as I want you now. Are you okay?" His words are a mere formality. I think we both know I'm good with this, but I answer obediently anyway.

"Green."

As soon as the word leaves my mouth he moves to the side, adjusting something on the back of the cross. It slowly tilts and my feet leave the floor as the weight of my body shifts, then finally settles as I lie flat against the horizontal surface.

I'm now a table.

Settling in beside me, Jake rubs my back, then cups my breast as I suck in a breath. The slightest movements cause new jolts of pain to shoot through me from the clamps biting my nipples.

His fingers brush against the little metal clasps and I whimper in release to the pressure that's been building inside of me.

"Your sounds are intoxicating." His lowered voice draws my attention to him as he checks my chest to make sure I'm positioned around the thin middle section of the cross and I am not lying directly on the clamps.

Then standing back up, he tugs at the small chain across my back pulling the clamps in unison, and I gift him a hiss as he chuckles in response.

"Lift your head."

Arching my back as best as I can, I raise my head up and with another latch, the upper section of the cross is closed, leaving me lying flat with my arms directly above my head as though it has become a capital I now.

"Relax. Take your time now. I'll be back in a moment."

I release my strength and lay my head against the bench. I could move my head to look around the room, but I don't. Instead I open my eyes and look into the small space between me and the table.

Since we spoke upstairs, I've wanted nothing but to get away for a few minutes. I wanted to return to myself and think. Now that I've finally been granted this time, I don't want it. My impatience is making me fidget in my restraints.

Everything about this room is an oxymoron. Wiggling my fingers, I feel the soft fabric of the cuffs against my skin. It's soothing, yet unyielding in how it holds me in place. The leather under me is smooth, but nothing that is about to happen on it will be gentle. The room is set up neatly but the chaos it contains is palpable.

A small shift of my hips sets off an electrified charge from my nipples as another nerve ending is lit up. So much pain from such a small thing.

How our bodies can flip on us like a switch has been turned on is incredible. I've giggled and cried in the last ten minutes, and I can't remember the last time I've done either of those things before tonight.

"Are you okay?" His gentle tone contradicts his firm touch as his hand settles on my back.

"Green." My mind follows the touch of his fingers as they glide over my skin instantly calming me. It's an odd sensation as I don't know what to expect now, but he is near me and I take comfort in that.

Jake moves the chain attached to the clamps higher up my back, resting them near the back of my neck. Then he trails his fingers over my back and down towards my rear.

He takes his time to squeeze each cheek, then repeats the motion a few more times. Each time I become a little more complacent under his touch, and as I shift my hip to offer my butt to him for his next grab, he puts me back in my place with a firm smack, jerking me out of my serenity and sending a wave of shock to my nipples as I jolt.

"I've told you, you need to learn how to expect the unexpected." His chastising is punctuated by four more smacks to my ass in no particular order, throwing me off guard.

I let his lesson sink in.

He's right.

I have always expected things to go according to my plan. But I'm not in control here. I've handed it over to him, and I need to understand that tonight is going to go by his rules, not mine.

Lost in my self-actualizing thoughts, a different sensation creeps across my upper back. This time I choose to trust the unexpected and instead of panic, I let the feeling in without knowing what it is.

"It's called a flogger." I sigh at his words.

I've just decided I like floggers...a lot.

Another hit lands across my back but this feels too good to be painful. It almost feels like fingers are tapping at my muscles. Fingers that carry a dull sting each time, and heat seeps into me at each contact.

As the deep massage of the flogger continues my head feels light again. I drift in and out as I enjoy the physical sting of the flogger along with the emotional rush from these chemicals Jake told me about.

I allow myself to float with each contact as they become rhythmic on my back and I moan as I relax in my binds.

"There's your moan, little one. I told you you would moan for me."

Stopping his cycle of hits, Jake shifts down from me and gently dangles the flogger over my bottom, touching only the tips to my skin. He's no longer hitting me, and they tickle against the fleshy bits he just spanked with his hand.

I let out a delirious giggle and I'm immediately shut up by the deep thud of a new tool that seems to ricochet a fire deep inside of me.

I freeze in place, trying to trust and process this new sensation. I have a sinking feeling this is the part where the pain comes in.

"This is a wood paddle. That was a light tap to get your attention. I'll start slow. Are you okay?"

This is my moment of truth. From the tone in his question, this is where he expects things to stop or continue and if I'm okay with this, I'll be good to go until the end, or if I use my safe word, whichever *comes* first.

Pun intended, I snort to myself.

"Green."

I'm so green right now I could get lost in the grass. I giggle again at the ridiculous thought.

How am I still giggling?

A second hit makes solid contact and the sting following it is more prominent causing me to cough in surprise, but he doesn't ask if I'm okay again.

This is just how it's going to go now.

Every hit after increases in strength. As the paddle connects a sixth time I choke on a breath of air. Each time the paddle hits my heated ass, I move a little causing the clamps on my nipples to further do their job, and the different sensations are building up to a boiling point inside of me to the point that I've started to clench the muscles at the top of my thighs together to ease my need.

"Yell—" My own voice surprises me and I stop myself from finishing the word.

I'm close to crying.

He stills beside me, waiting.

Oddly enough, it isn't the worst pain I've felt, not even close, but I'm ready to sob.

I'm ready to open up and release everything I'm holding in, and this is why I'm ready to say the word, but I can't do this to myself. I don't run away from anything, let alone myself.

Taking a deep breath, I answer his question without him asking it.

"Green."

Without verbal confirmation, he steps back to me and lands a seventh spank. The intensity isn't as strong as the sixth, he's taken a small step back to test me.

I won't fail him.

I won't fail myself.

Two more hits find their mark, and my ass is on fire. I don't even know if he is still increasing in strength now because I only feel sting after heated sting as my nipples continue to ache as I react.

As the paddle hits again, I'm back to my choked out cry.

I'm dancing along the edge of what's left of my composure. I'm right there.

Another smack lands square on my buttocks and I'm done. As if that single motion was the key to the floodgates, the door is unlocked and I cry.

Sucking in air I attempt to breathe calmly, but my body shakes. My dam breaks and from it, my emotions flow. I'm crying for so many things, and right now I desperately, more than anything, want him to spank me while I am in tears and I have no idea why.

So I cry some more.

"Embrace your shame. This last one is going to hurt."

Shame.

Another new one for me and I've decided I have a love/hate relationship with paddles.

The paddle connects harshly against my skin, stripping everything from me. Drops run down my face, but it's not because of the pain.

I've held a lifetime of unnecessary weight, and it is draining out of me with each drop.

"There's your tears. I told you you would cry for me."

My limbs ache and I'm tired, but I want more. I want all of him.

A click echos through the cross I am lying on, and a flood of cold air chills my center as my legs are spread wide for him when he opens the lower half of the cross and locks it in place.

I sense him at my side, but he doesn't touch me so I lift my head to look up at him.

He looks the same, but he's not.

He offers me no comfort with his smile.

He's focused, hungry.

His eyes meet my own as he removes his shirt exposing the hard ridges I knew were underneath.

Bending over to remove his pants, his cock bounces straight up as he stands and I understand his hunger as though it is my own.

I'm needy for him, and I lick my lips shamelessly in front of him.

"Head down." I obey his words, dropping my head to the table. I'm running out of energy anyway so this is a sweet mercy for me.

As he moves the tiny chain into its original spot on my back, my nipples pull again, but the pain isn't as strong. I imagine my nerve endings have almost given up by now.

His touch is cold against my throbbing ass and a soft squeeze draws a whimper from me. My mewls turn to moans as his hand slides between the crevice of my ass and into my slick folds as he rubs back and forth through my slick.

After the pain, this feels more intense than the first time

he touched me, and I lift my ass to try to give him more access.

Need swells within me as he controls me, and I want a repeat of the first orgasm he gave me.

As if answering my prayers with a firm *no*, a sharp sting lands right between my legs, and I jerk against my binds in response.

"This is a crop. Have you started expecting things again, my sweet little angel?"

I stay silent.

I'm mad at him because I'm not getting what I want and I'm mad because he's right, again.

My patience is wearing thin.

I'm over the moon gone. My need is beginning to fester inside of me like a caged animal being poked and taunted.

A second, direct hit to my pussy and the pain sharpens. It hurts, but it doesn't.

Another oxymoron.

Rough fingers slide back along my pussy and I groan my pleasure again.

A third tap on my pussy and pain no longer registers. Neither does pleasure. It's something in between.

My head swirls as he alternates between the touch of his hand and the slap of his crop, and I'm close to crying again when a soothing wetness moves along my pussy from my clit almost to my tight ring and a carnal cry floats around the room.

Closing my mouth, I realize that was me.

"You taste perfect. Fuck." His tongue runs the length of me a second time, and my wanton moans match his depraved growl as I drown in the sensation of being consumed by him.

His fingers dig into my ass as he pulls me into his

mouth. Thoughts of me being restrained to this cross as he feasts on me fill my head driving me to the brink of insanity.

I want to tell him I'm going to come again, but he's told me not to speak. The muscles in my legs and stomach tense as I prepare for my next orgasm to hit me and he stops.

Releasing his fingers from my ass, he stands and lands a solid spank on my cheek.

I growl at him, and he chuckles in response as he moves to the head of the cross.

Another click opens my arms and my head dangles down between the space left as the top of the cross spreads wide for him.

Lifting my head, I land inches away from his bulging cock. His musky scent hits me.

A drop of precum sits at the tip of his shaft and I lick my lips in a heady haze.

How have I been turned into this creature lying here, bound to a cross and aching for everything this man will give me?

"Now it's time to beg for me."

He knows.

He's reading me like I'm an open book, but I don't care.

"P-please, Jake," I whimper. "Please. I need to taste you. Please feed me your cock."

A smirk returns to his face as his finger touches my cheek and runs down and across my mouth. My desperation takes hold, and I stick out my tongue to taste the saltiness on his rough finger while I keep my eyes on his. His smile falters, and he swallows hard.

I know as much as he has me, I have him too.

Pulling his hand back, he tangles his fingers into the top of my hair and holds my head up as he steps closer to me.

He tastes salty on the tip of my tongue, and as I open

my mouth to take in his length, a sweetness hits me as well. This is the first time since he strapped me in that I've wanted to be released. I want to consume him completely but I can't.

He moves as he wishes.

He's guiding me like I'm his toy.

I am.

I open my mouth to accommodate whatever he needs, and he moans as he hits the back of my throat over and over again and I choke around his thick girth.

Lost in the tempo of his thrusts I settle myself as he uses my mouth when he suddenly stills deep inside, then slowly pulls out.

Releasing a heavy sigh of his own, he tugs on my wrist as he reaches for my cuff.

"I'm releasing your restraints, hold onto the hooks and don't let go until I tell you to." He moves to my second cuff.

He walks out of my line of sight and stops somewhere behind me, between my spread legs. His hands once again squeeze my ass just as he did when he first hooked me into this contraption. He needs my fleshy cheeks, pulling them apart and revealing all of my sins.

Sliding his fingers between my lips he dips one finger into my opening and pulls out, spreading my juices around my pussy and slowly trailing his finger over my perineum toward my ass, then he repeats the motion a few more times.

With my legs bound wide, I have no choice but to enjoy the sensation and my attention is focused on that single motion.

"You've been such a good girl for me, Ahna." He draws out my name like he did when we first spoke. "Now it's time for your reward. Tell me you want me to fuck you." His hand keeps moving along my core as my head fills with delirious excitement.

"I—I want you to fuck me, Jake. I want that so badly." My words pour out of me. My complete truth. I want nothing more than to get railed by him on this cross.

"I know, Ahna. I know." In one motion he answers every wish I've ever had as he pulls me back to him by my hips, opening me further. As he pushes his whole length deep inside of me in one long motion, my body stretches around him.

I hang onto the hooks for dear life as he continues to pull me towards him.

Our groans join together in unison as he pulls back and pushes in a second time, and I'm ready to burst wide open for him.

There is nothing about this that is gentle, yet it is the most beautiful thing I've ever felt.

I close my eyes to let everything outside of my sight hit me. I'm overwhelmed by the pleasure of his fucking matched with the painful reminder as his hips slap against my reddened ass.

Reminding me to expect the unexpected, his palm connects with my cheek and my ass jiggles for him as I continue to bounce on his cock.

Embracing my salacious need, I revel in my lust and a devilish sneer graces my lips as I moan my eternal gratitude to him for setting me free.

His fingers move up the back of my neck and fist my hair at the base of my skull as he continues his onslaught, and from the edge of my rapture, I feel it.

His hand grips my ass once, then slides into my crevice, landing just outside of my tight rim. He pushes his thumb, testing it slowly as he continues to pound into me and I relax, opening myself to him.

My juices make it easy for him to slide around my tight hole and as he pushes into me, his thumb breaches my back opening as he rubs in and out of my outer muscle.

"Let go of the hooks." My brain immediately complies and I release my grip.

Holding my ass with his thumb deep inside of me with one hand, his second hand pulls my head back and I arch my back and prop myself up on the cross with my hands as his thrusts increase in strength and speed.

"Touch yourself. I want you to play with yourself."

My abyss is heading toward me at record speed and I shift my weight as I shove my hand between my legs and begin to rub my clit furiously for him.

His thumb slips from my ass, and his hand moves to my hips for a moment.

"I'm going to remove your clamps now. You will not come until I say so." His words don't phase me in the least. I'm pretty sure my nipples have gone numb as I haven't felt anything from them in a—

"HOLY SHIT!" I scream into the room completely forgetting his rule.

As the feeling rushes back into my nipple, so does the pain and it mixes with the pleasure we are both currently riding out.

"No coming. Are you okay?" He makes no move to slow his thrusts and my patience breaks.

"Green. Fucking green, dammit."

His laugh is triumphant.

As his hand crosses my body, I hesitate. I want time to prepare for the next wave of pain, but there's no way in hell

I'm saying anything other than *green* now so I keep my lips pinched together tightly until—

A shrill cry tears from me when he removes the second clamp, and light flashes into my vision as though someone just turned the lights to the room up, then back down again.

As I gasp for air, his palms run over my raw nipples attempting to soothe them down then with a tight clench of hair, he pulls my head back toward him, growling into my ear.

"Keep touching my things, Ahna." He commands, and I notice I've stopped playing with myself to brace for the pain.

My stomach knots tight as he pounds fiercely in and out of me, and I shove my hand back to my swollen clit, continuing to touch myself for him.

An energy pulses through my veins leaving me with, what I'm sure is, a false sense of strength as we both begin to fuck in our basest forms.

Clawing against the leather, my other hand rubs feverishly over the most sensitive area on my clit and I prepare to step off the edge into my abyss.

"You have a question, Ahna. Ask it." He commands as he barrels along with me.

I don't hesitate. "May I come. Please, Jake."

I'm already past the point of no return. I will do anything to come for him right now.

"You're mine, Ahna. Tell me who you belong to." He demands as he pounds into me, grabbing one of my bouncing tits with his free hand.

"You. I belong to you. I'm all yours. Please, Jake. May I come?"

His answer is close to becoming irrelevant, but I want to hear his words as I fly apart for him.

"You are all mine and I'm yours. You may come, precious."

My life leaves my body as I let go.

I feel it. Everything I am is his. I've given him control and he's set me free.

All pain leaves my body as wave after wave of pure energy hit me, and I open myself to the world around me in a long drawn out wail.

In the same vein, he is mine.

He groans profanities as he follows me into euphoria, and his thrusts end with one final push as he floods deep inside of me.

Wrapping his arms around my chest, he leans over top of me to hold me tight in an embrace as our adrenaline collectively leaves us.

After a moment of catching our breath, he brushes his hands over my ankles and, one by one, I'm released from the cuffs as he turns me over and cradles me in his arms, carrying me across the room and onto the bed.

As he slides in beside me and pulls the covers up, I close my eyes for a moment and allow the sound of his heart to calm me.

CHAPTER 3
JAKE

Ahna's gentle breaths against my chest as she rests her head on me is a sharp contrast to the aggressive taking only moments before, and it feels incredible.

From the moment I saw her standing on my porch, I knew she would be mine. I just didn't know it would happen so quickly.

Our connection took on a life of its own and consumed us both.

There's still so much I want to know about her, and I'm not ready for her to leave here in search for the new life she was speaking about.

I'll be her new life.

"Are you okay?" I comb my fingers through her hair, and she moans at the contact.

"Green." She answers with a hint of humour in her tone. "I'm okay."

She is the sweetest creature I've ever met yet she answered my need so divinely. I always thought I would end up with someone more hardened.

"Okay, good. I have to be honest. I thought my room would scare you off." Her body tenses and I wonder if she's replaying all of our sins.

"I don't scare easily." She lifts her hand, drawing something on my chest with her slender finger.

"This sounds crazy but I don't want you to leave here on Monday. You said yourself you don't have anything to go back to. Stay with me for a while."

Now that I say it out loud, the desperation in my voice is obvious, but I don't care.

I have nothing to lose anyway.

The truth is I have nothing to go back to either, and her lying here beside me is more than I could have ever hoped for.

"I'd like that, but I have some things I need to sort out first." The promise in her answer makes me hopeful I'll be able to explore more of her.

"Anything you need."

As I wrap my arm around her little body my mind wanders back over the evening.

Everything about her flowed so effortlessly. Her willingness to step out of her boundaries. Her trust and her submission to me were like something out of a "Fairy tale." I say the word out loud then chuckle to myself.

She stills. "Pardon me?"

"Oh, nothing. I was just thinking. Maybe I can make you believe in fairy tales after all."

"I never said I didn't believe in fairy tales. I just meant that it's hard to trust the devil's tale when it always gets the most important detail wrong." She says confidently against my chest.

"And what detail is that?" Lifting my head off the pillow I pull her up to get a better look at her face.

The room twists around me, and I blink to correct my vision as her sweet head tilts up to meet my gaze.

From behind jet black eyes, her voice tenderly answers me as the room fades away.

"My gender of course, silly."

About Luna

Luna Kayne is a romance author located in Canada. She writes dark, explicit, romantic suspense with a hint of humor and angst. Her men are dominant and often stubborn, and her women are usually underestimated. As for tropes and sub-genres, nothing is off the table.

Luna Kayne is the pen name of author *Sheri Landry* who writes non-romance action thrillers and has won awards for her writing under both names. Gardening relaxes her, she dislikes long winters, and she doesn't understand how commas work.

You can learn more and find her books at LunaKayne.com.

facebook.com/LunaKayne

twitter.com/LunaKayne

instagram.com/LunaKayne

bookbub.com/profile/luna-kayne